THE WIZARD NEXT DOOR

by **Peter Glassman**

illustrated by **Steven Kellogg**

Morrow Junior Books
New York

Colored inks, watercolors, and acrylics were used for the full-color artwork. The text type is 18-point Caxton.

Library of Congress Cataloging-in-Publication Data
Glassman, Peter. The wizard next door / by Peter Glassman ; illustrated by Steven Kellogg.
p. cm. Summary: A child notices some magical things about the man who moves in next door—but no one else does. ISBN 0-688-10645-5.—ISBN 0-688-10646-3 (lib. bdg.) [1. Imagination—Fiction. 2. Magic—Fiction.] I. Kellogg, Steven, ill. II. Title. PZ7.G481437Wi 1993 [E]—dc20
92-21562 CIP AC

For
Larry G. Myers,
who first showed me the magic
and
James M. Carey,
who keeps it alive
—P. G.

To Tatia the Great,
with love
—S. K.

Mr. Myers is a wizard.

I know he is.

But no one believes me.

When he moved in, I saw
all sorts of strange things.

But when I tried to show Mom, she just said,

"What an imagination you have!"

One day I saw Mr. Myers making
a magic potion in his backyard.

I showed Dad, but all he saw was Mr. Myers cooking hot dogs on his barbeque.

Mr. Myers has very strange pets.

I tried to show them to my sister,
but she just said they were "neat."

From then on I watched Mr. Myers carefully.

He has the greatest way of putting his books back on the shelf.

And he really knows how to get
rid of unwanted visitors.

And traffic jams never bother him.

One day my teacher was sick.

Mr. Myers was our teacher for the day.

When the terrible Turner twins
tried to use their squirt guns on him,
they got a real surprise.

And Cathy found that making faces
behind his back…

wasn't a good idea.

Mr. Myers was a great teacher.

His stories really came to life.

And math was never so much fun.

But the next day, no one else remembered
that anything strange had happened.
They all thought I was pretending.

It made me mad! "Why doesn't anyone else
see your magic?" I yelled.

"Because they don't want to," he answered.
"Then why do I see it?" I asked.

"Because you're looking for magic," he said.
"And there is so much more I can show you!"

Now I go over to Mr. Myers's house every day.

I help him clean up his laboratory…

and help take care of his pets.

But best of all, Mr. Myers is teaching me magic.

Now I can do all sorts of amazing things.

Setting the table for dinner is really easy.

And so is washing my dog, Sparky.

Raking leaves takes no time at all.

And I'm never late for school!